T0002355

Surugamonkey

# BAKEMONOGATARI

OH!GREAT

ORIGINAL STORY:
NISIOISIN

ORIGINAL CHARACTER
DESIGN: VOFAN

4

MAIN CHARACTERS
Koyomi Araragi
A boy who was attacked by a vampire. Accepts Hitagi's confession of love and is currently dating her.
Hitagi Senjogahara
A girl whose weight was once stolen by a "crab." Tells Koyomi how she feels when they send Mayoi on her way.
Mayoi Hachikuji
A "Lost Snail" who tries to visit her mother's house but can never arrive. Finally makes it home after Koyomi and friends save her.
Tsubasa Hanekawa
The infallible class president in Koyomi's class who was once bewitched by a "cat." Dealing with problems at home.
Karen Araragi / Tsukihi Araragi
Koyomi's two younger siblings who are known as "Tsuganoki Second Middle School's Fire Sisters." Rouses Koyomi from bed each morning. Karen is the older sister. Tsukihi is the younger one.

Mayoi Hachikuji is a "Lost Snail" who can never reach her mother's house. Koyomi Araragi enlists the help of Hitagi Senjogahara and aberrations expert Mèmè Oshino, and somehow manages to bring the Lost Snail back home. After that, Koyomi accepts Hitagi's declaration of love and they start going out. Now that the case has been solved and a new relationship has begun, things are finally starting to look up...

Chapter 3

# Suruga Monkey

BOOK DESIGN VEIA

Here's the epi-logue. Or maybe
KOYO-MIII! WAKE UP!
the punchline to this "snail aberration."
The next day,
I was roused from bed
GHURK!
Flying double-team dogpile!!
by my sisters Karen and Tsukihi as usual. It seemed ...

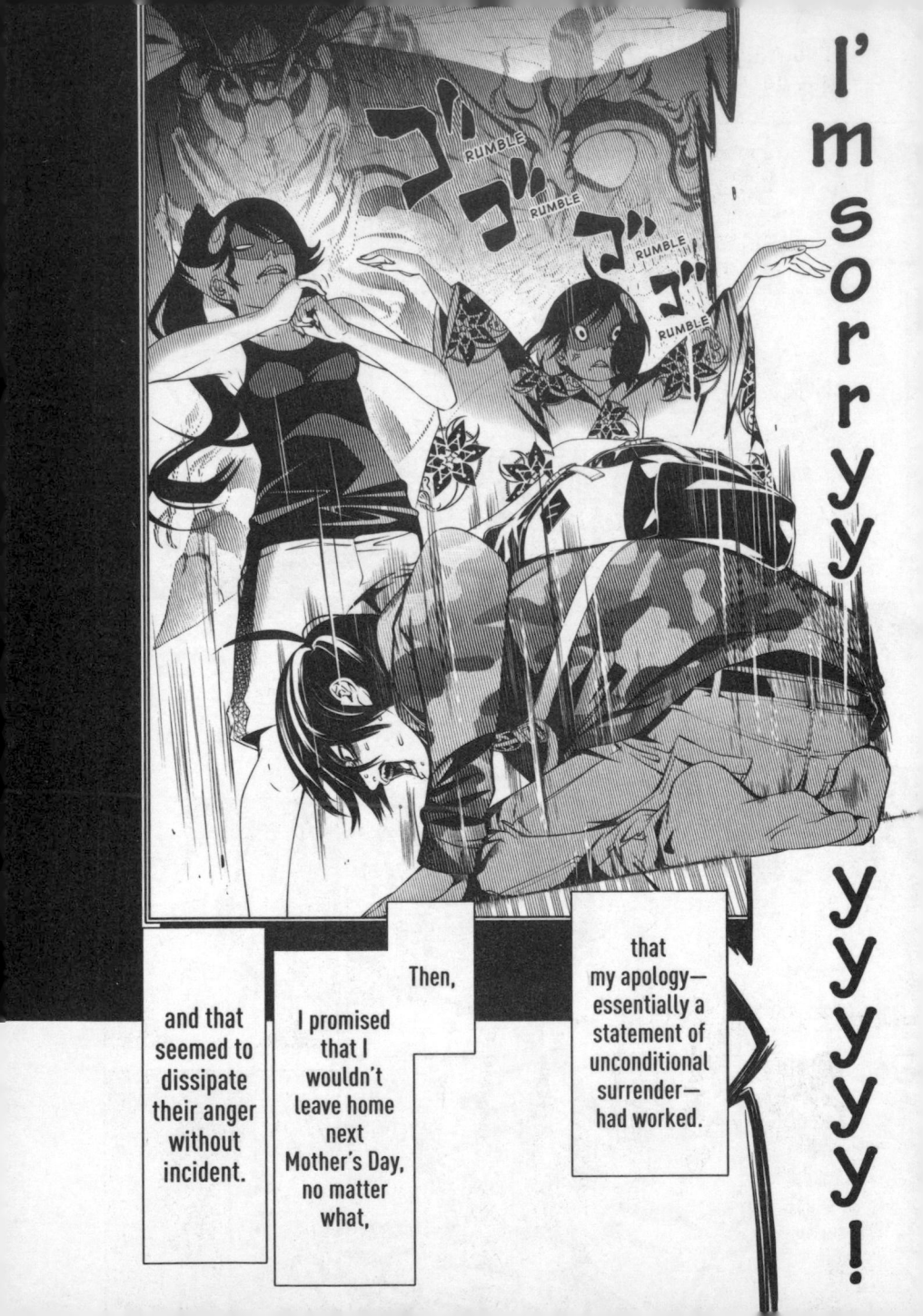
I'm sorryyyyyyyyy!
ゴゴゴゴ
RUMBLE
RUMBLE
RUMBLE
RUMBLE
that my apology—essentially a statement of unconditional surrender—had worked.
Then,
I promised that I wouldn't leave home next Mother's Day, no matter what,
and that seemed to dissipate their anger without incident.

Two weeks later.
May 29, 5:20 p.m.
SHAAAA
...
Crap ...!
PEEK
WHAA ?!!
GYAKKING

AH.
MISTER AH-HA-HA-GI.
...
Don't turn me into some sidekick who takes his name from his cluelessness, Hachikuji.
It makes me sound like a total loser.
Well, I think it's cute.
It might be surprisingly fitting.

I'M GLAD TO SEE YOU'RE DOING WELL!
HOW HAVE THINGS BEEN? ANY *INCIDENTS* SINCE LAST TIME?
That kind of thing isn't common.
It's been peaceful. Quiet, even.
そわそわ FIDGET
そわ FIDGET
HM? IS SOMETHING THE MATTER?!
No, no. It's nothing.
How about you, Mayoi? I thought you fully passed on to the afterlife...
Huh?
Well, the thing is ...
...
Oh. Um...

ドンドンドンドンドン
TRRRA-TA-TA-TA-TA-TA-TAAA
THANKS TO YOU, MISTER ARARAGI,
I'VE BEEN PROMOTED FROM RESIDUAL GHOST TO WANDERING GHOST!!
UP

IT'S WHAT YOU MIGHT CALL SKIPPING TWO GRADES !!
...
Wha ...?
I didn't know that was possible ...
Who knew.
I don't know if it's frivolous or barely thought-out...
So every-thing's fine and dandy...
but even Oshino would faint if he heard this.
Though I wouldn't mind seeing that, to be honest...
Wandering Ghost Lv.3
unknown Lv.?
Residual Ghost Lv.51
But... what's between a residual ghost and a wandering one...?
Any-way,
Job change

what is the matter, Mister Araragi?
You seemed to be in quite the hurry!
Oh,
I'm just stopping by home.
Yeah.
I have a skills test coming up.
"Just stopping by"? So you'll be out again later?
Your skills, Mister Araragi ...?
So your abilities, your very *worth*, will face a moment of truth?!
...IT'S NOT THAT DRAMATIC!

...I'd honestly be happier if you just called me stupid.
Well, your mental difficulties are rather outstanding.
You really are a washout, aren't you...?
I'm seriously gonna be in a bad spot if I bungle this skills test.
The moment of truth... is simply whether I'll be able to graduate.
Instead of calling herself stupid, she merely said she didn't have "the best grades." I feel like she's trying to trick me...
...
Don't worry. I don't have the best grades either, so we're the same! Totes in the same boat.
that you're going to study at the library or a cram school... or something?
Premium Festival
So you're saying

I'm going to a study session at Senjogahara's.
...
Ya know, since she gets some of the best marks in my grade...
You remember her, right? The one with the long hair...
A study session ?!?
TWITCH
O-... O-... Of course, I do.
Miss Senjogahara... That... tsundere... with the sharp eyes— no,
TREMBLE
TREMBLE
TREMBLE
that endlessly tolerant woman who carried me on her back the entire time as she showed me the way home...
WHAT'S WITH THE EMBELLISHED MEMORIES!?!

YOU'VE ENTERED INTO A LOVERS' CON-TRACT!
THAT'S THE WORST WAY TO PHRASE IT!!!
Oh...? But... That's right! If I'm not mistaken, you and Miss Senjogahara are... well, how do I put it...?
Whew.
WOBB
So, in other words, aren't your studies no more than a pretext
Hmm... But wait, Mister Araragi.
Transaction Flow
Love
B
A
Money, praise, preferential choice
Pay
Exclusive transaction
In that case, how about "trans-action" instead?
THAT SOUNDS EVEN WORSE!!
A LOVERS' TRANS-ACTION.

There's something way off about her vocabulary.
And what is she doing with her fingers...?
Ca-ress-es...?
for you to end up trading caress-es?
Visiting your lover's home right before a skills test that will ascertain if you can graduate
is nothing short of suicidal, is it not?
It seems that this grade schooler thinks I'm a pretty big idiot.
...
I'm getting the feeling that I'm gonna have to bust you up sooner or later.

Don't play gotcha when you haven't even gotten me.
SHUT UP.
SMAK
What exactly are you seeking from my grade-schooler body?
Bust me up? Are you referring to my chest? Or perhaps my rear end?
MUKI
Wait, Mister Araragi.
gotta go, Hachikuji.
Well,
Listen, it's gonna be fine. Senjogahara's mega-strict when it comes to this stuff.
I think I'm going to wander around this area for a while.
Naoetsu Town Area Map

SO IF YOU SEE ME, PLEASE DO SPEAK TO ME.
So, I guess I
Hachikuji really said that.
Those words came from her, of all people.

Re-
zoning
Thank you
for your
cooperation
this
must
be
quite
the
won-
derful
story.

As
good
as it
gets.

Bye ...
Talk later, Hanekawa ...
KLANK
K-KLONK
KLINK
SKREEK

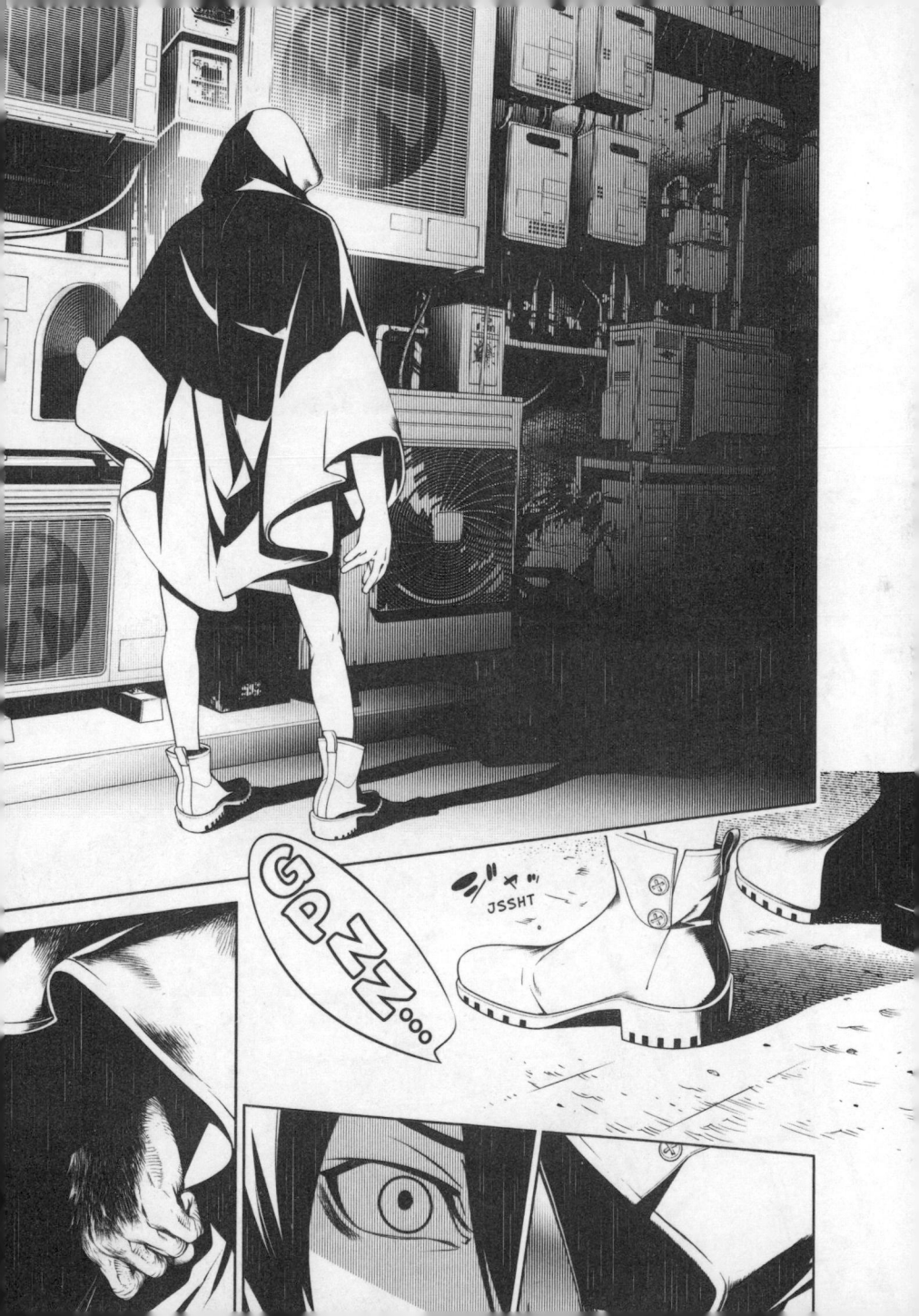
GRZZ...
JSSHT

WHAM!

# BAKEMONOGATARI

## 03: Suruga Monkey

DOOMF
ZZAK
BSHH
... That ...
... was close ...!!
I...
know what this is...!

DSCHH
Er, never mind. I don't have a clue.
I don't even know why I'm being attacked...
but ...
on "spring break,"
I encountered *this feeling* again and again ...!!!

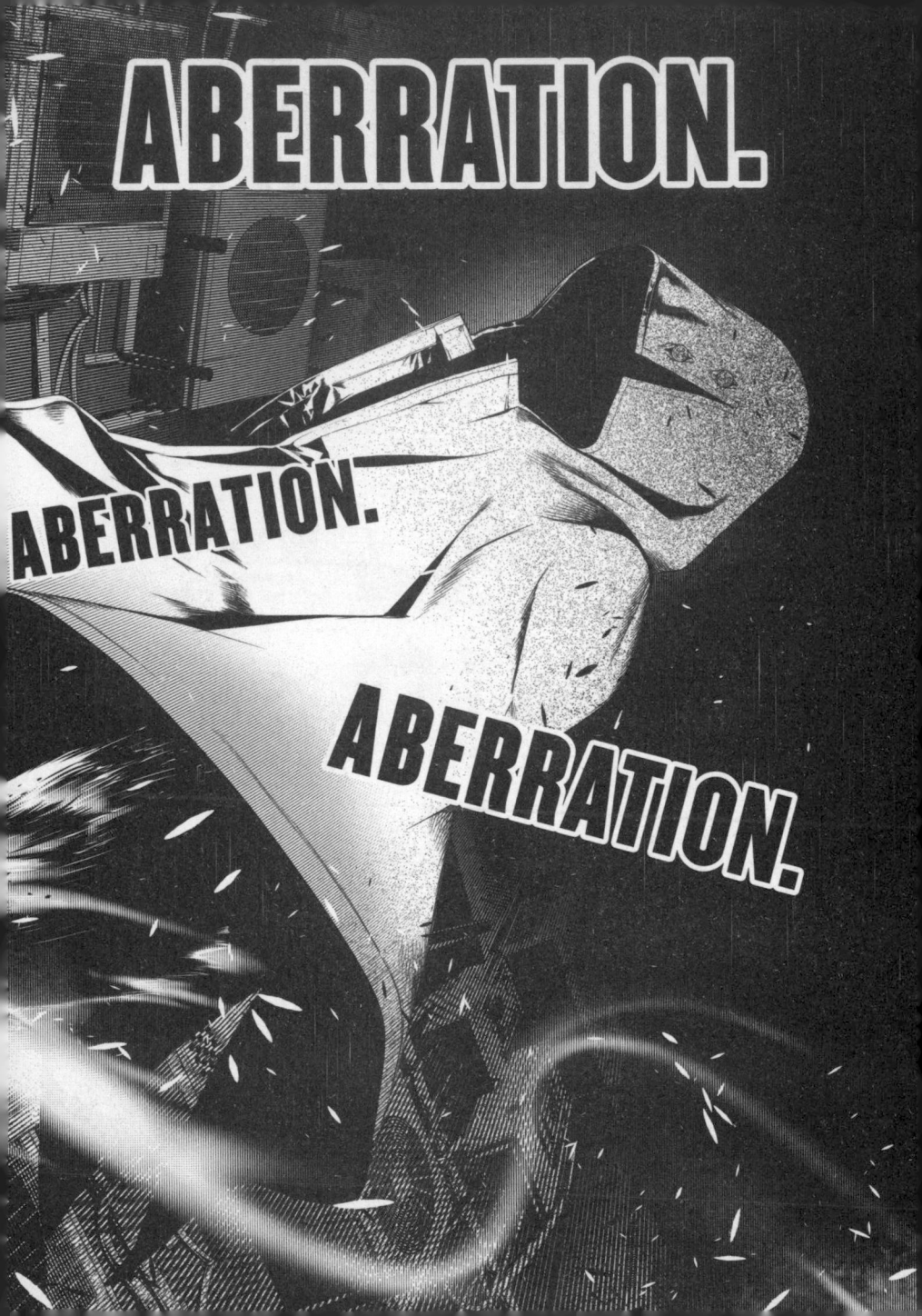
ABERRATION.
ABERRATION.
ABERRATION.

ABERRATION.

There's a maze of alleys behind me.
Can I flee ...?
so I'm used to this.
I, too, have some experience under my belt...
SHUDDER
No ...
I can't.
There should have been 5 to 6 yards between us
before it attacked ...
I don't have the courage to turn my back on this thing...!
TREMBLE
TREMBLE
TREMBLE
SHFF
SHFF

but I didn't see it ... at all.
and it just so happened to miss me.
I thought I was done for and leapt out of the way,
Though my dear, precious bike was forever lost in my place...
Escaping from its absurdly strong legs
is impos-sible...
PA-KRAK
WHOA!

CHNK
BOOOM
BSHH
I retract
my previous state-ment.
KRAK
KRAK
KRAK
KRAK
Not to this.
I'm not used to it.

GRRRKK
Now's my chance !
!!
KREAK
BAM
GNNK
KRRCH

KRAK
KRAK
KRAK
KRAAASH

ZHMM
KRAK
THWAK
I don't ...
understand...
THWAK
THWAK

None of this.
This wicked power.
These ungodly abilities.
ZSHHH
On spring break, I saw the King of Aberrations.
Compared to Kiss-Shot Acerola-Orion Heart-Under-Blade's nonsensical power,
this is something I can fathom ...
but still.

Meeting Oshino, a vampire, a crab, and a snail
has taught me one thing ...
KLOMP
KLOMP
KLOMP
TREMBLE
TREMBLE
DRIBB
GRRT
"There is a reason for every aberration."
SLIP
BSHH
Haah
Haah
Which means there's a logical reason why this thing's attacking me...!
There should be, I think... But I have no idea what it is.
ZHK
ZHK
ZHK

Haah
What happened today...? Who did I see?
What did I talk about ... and with *whom*?!
Haa
Re-mem-ber...
Haah
GHURK
DRIBB
C'mon, think...! One of them must have a clue that'll get me out of this alive...!!!
My little sisters.
Hachi-kuji.
Senjo-gahara.
Hane-kawa.

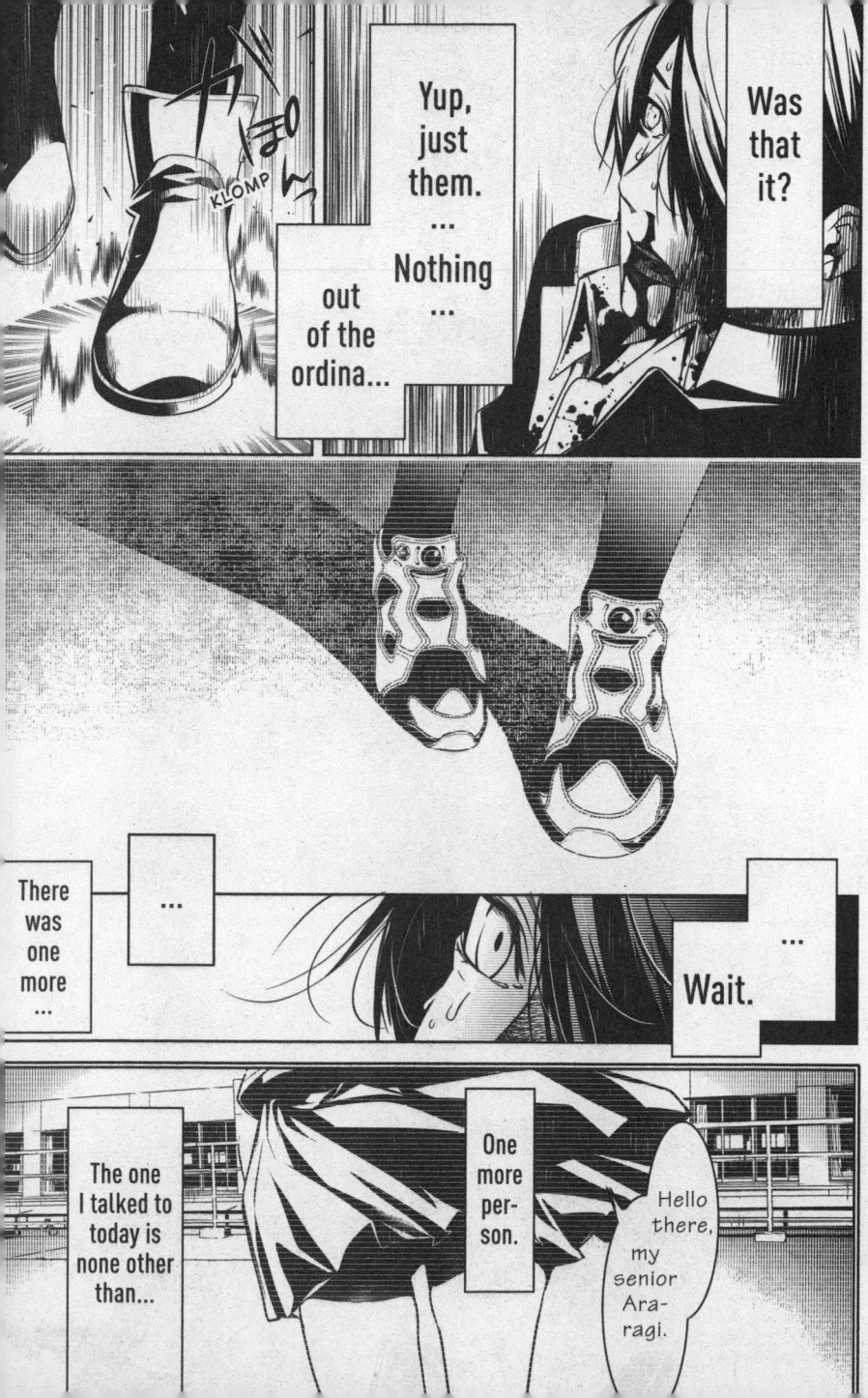
Was that it?
Yup, just them. ... Nothing ... out of the ordina...
KLOMP
...
Wait.
...
There was one more ...
One more person.
Hello there, my senior Araragi.
The one I talked to today is none other than...

What a coinci-dence.

It
looks
like

I have to talk about Suruga Kanbaru.

I'VE NEVER HEARD OF SUCH A CONTRIVED COINCIDENCE!
YOU CLEARLY SPRINTED RIGHT TO ME!!
... What is it ...?!
Oh, nothing. I was just engraving your words deep in my heart so I'd never forget them.
"I've never heard of such a contrived coincidence"—
A perfect line for the occasion. That's what I call razor wit. I should have expected as much from you.

YES, YOU'RE RIGHT. I DID COME CHASING AFTER YOU.
GRIN
The school's mega-celebrity and star of the basketball team,
I know...
Suruga Kanbaru, was stalking me.

SKRRK
SKRRK
SKREE
VICTORY
SGRRK
Suruga Kan-baru ...

BAKEMONOGATARI

can
fly.

She is the undisputed star of the team since her first year, and the current team captain.
Our love makes you invincible
SURUGA
YEAAAH!
You "Kan" do it Kanbaru!!
あがんばる!!
神原
Since Naoetsu High is a prep school,
WHEEZ
WHEEZ
No more...
we weren't so good when it comes to athletics.
SLAM
NAOETSU
But Kanbaru took our weak little basketball team and turned it into a national powerhouse ...
CONGRATS ON MAKING IT TO THE ATIONAL TOURNAMENT
Girls' Basketball Team
Naoetsu High School Student Council
all on her own.

ASAURI NEWS
The media descended on her after each match.
You gave another impressive performance today.
Aw, shucks.
And most of all,
she has a cheerful personality that no one can hate.
Sure, the position and the role I play means that I stand out, but this is all thanks to everyone else.
Basketball isn't a forgiving sport where you can count on any single person to win the game.
The endless praise I get should be shared by the whole team.

where people watched her and whispered about every move she made. She wasn't just a celebrity, but a *mega*-celebrity.
It got to the point
"If you want to know what Kanbaru had for breakfast, just ask anyone. They'll know."
Even though I stayed far away from gossip, I knew a lot about this girl one grade below me.
PSSHHH
I'd never gotten within a 5-yard—no, not even a 30- or 50-yard radius of her.
That knowledge was only a one-way thing, of course.

She and I lived in entirely different worlds.
She and I were entirely different types of people.
If I grow my hair down to here, maybe my summer uniform can hide my wound...
There was, of course, no reason for her to know about me...
or so I thought.
That was what I'd assumed.
TUP
TUP
TUP
TUP

BWAH
SKRRRK
スリキュキュ

If it isn't my senior Araragi.
HISSS
Hello there. What a coincidence.
Kanbaru started talking to me out of nowhere.
She spoke as if we'd always been good friends—like nothing was off.
That was on May 16.
I'VE NEVER HEARD OF SUCH A CONTRIVED COINCIDENCE!
The stalking started there—then came May 19.
Ha ha ha. Yes, you're right.
I did come chasing after you.
I know ...
AH, SO YOU DID KNOW! I SHOULD HAVE EXPECTED THAT MUCH FROM A SENIOR LIKE YOU, ARARAGI.
SO, ANYTHING A FLEDGLING LIKE ME TRIES TO PULL IS TRANSPARENT TO SOMEONE OF YOUR CALIBER, I TAKE IT! IT IS AWKWARD, AND I COULDN'T FEEL ANY MORE EMBARRASSED, BUT I AM DULY IMPRESSED!!
HA HA
HA HA
はっはっ
はっはっ

...
Don't you have ... practice ...?
Should you ... even be here ...?
God, this is awkward ...
No Unauthorized Visitors
For reasons unknown she's been chasing me around ever since... and I spend my days running and hiding at full-speed.
It's not that I don't like her. I mean, what right does a washout like me have to say anything about the star of the academy?
Yes, it's that I just don't know how to deal with this stuff...plain and simple.
BSHT
A-HA! SO ASTUTE, AS I'VE COME TO EXPECT! YOU'RE LIKE THE HERO OF A DETECTIVE STORY WHO NEVER MISSES THE SLIGHTEST DISCREPANCY!
WHY, YOU'D GIVE PHILIP MARLOWE A RUN FOR HIS MONEY, A BAREFOOT RUN!

I'd never want to read a novel with a protagonist capable of giving detectives a barefoot run for their money with observations that lame...
Anyone would think that.
You're the captain of a national-level basketball team...
after all.
Mm.
But see?
My arm is like this now, so...
Right...
She sprained it during a workout or something...

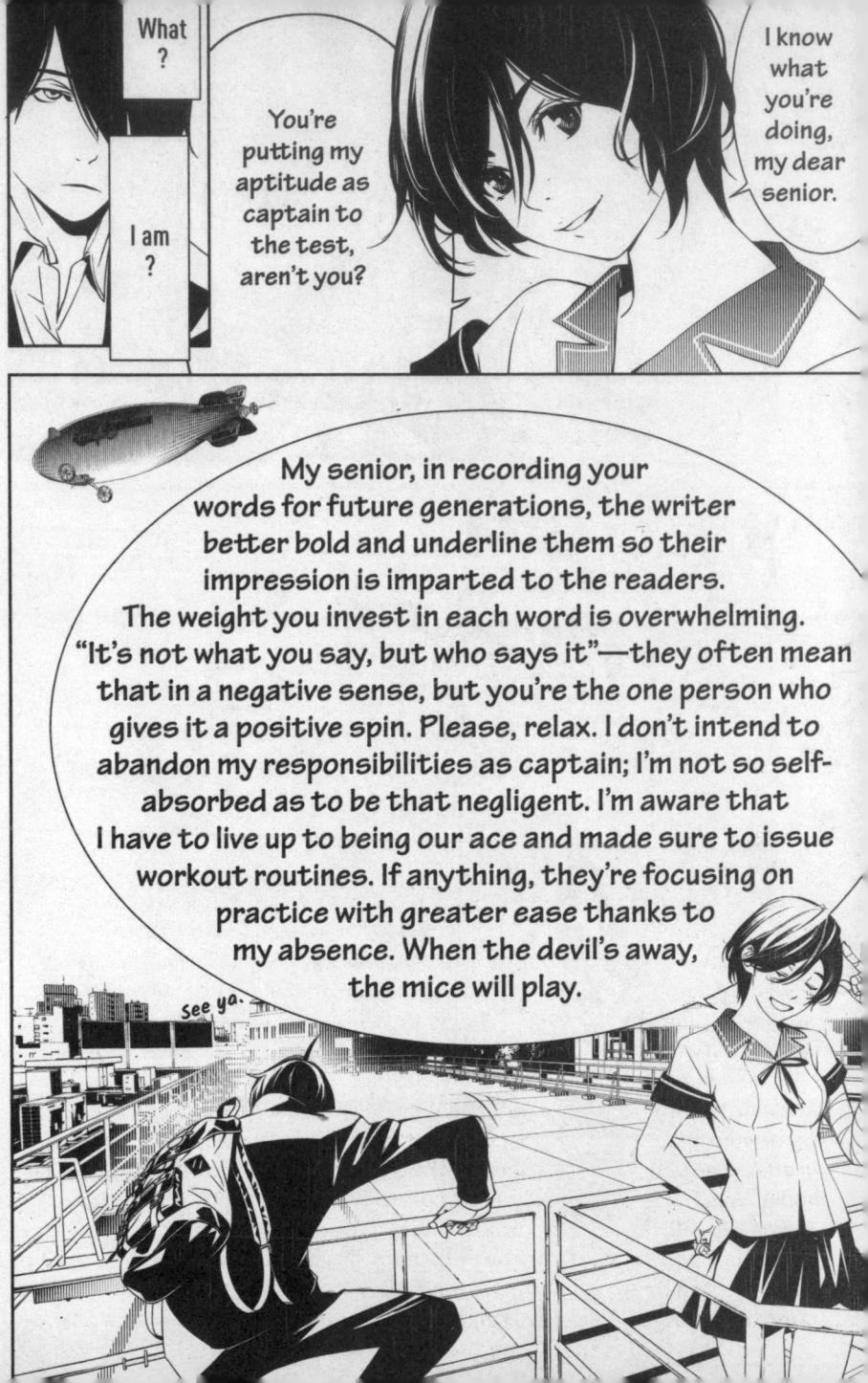
What ?
I am ?
You're putting my aptitude as captain to the test, aren't you?
I know what you're doing, my dear senior.
My senior, in recording your words for future generations, the writer better bold and underline them so their impression is imparted to the readers. The weight you invest in each word is overwhelming. "It's not what you say, but who says it"—they often mean that in a negative sense, but you're the one person who gives it a positive spin. Please, relax. I don't intend to abandon my responsibilities as captain; I'm not so self-absorbed as to be that negligent. I'm aware that I have to live up to being our ace and made sure to issue workout routines. If anything, they're focusing on practice with greater ease thanks to my absence. When the devil's away, the mice will play.
See ya.

Even a sports team is just a club activity for students. Moreover, ours is a prep school. At the end of the day, an extracurricular is a way for us teens to have some memories, so fun, free, and friendly does it. Even so, most of my betters wouldn't bother to have anything to do with me, but not only are you looking out for my relationships, you're even thinking of my teammates. I feel bad for making you so concerned. Such depth of character expands my own horizons—to think that you'd even play the villain for the basketball team's sake. Only someone who truly cares about his juniors could go that far. I've never met a person like you before, sir.

So what do you want from me, Kanbaru?
!!
I was hoping to hear your thoughts on the unfolding political situation in Russia.
I KNOW NOTHING ABOUT IT!!!

Now that's what it means to be broad-minded.
How generous of you. I didn't expect to be forgiven so easily. There is simply no way someone with your gravitas didn't find my remark superficial, but you let it go without so much as hinting at your displeasure.
Sure, I really don't care at this point...
We can put the topic off until tomorrow in that case, if that's all right with you.
Well, you are a busy man. I can see how you might not have the time to read the paper in the morning. I apologize, I should have thought of it before blabbering so inconsiderately.
I see.
THAT I COULD COME TO LIKE YOU EVEN MORE!
YOU KNOW, I NEVER THOUGHT
SMAK
HA-HAH
No need for gratitude! I'm just letting you know how I feel!!
...
HA HA HA
I see... thanks...
...

LIBRARY
...
Later, Kanbaru.
OH!! HOLD ON,
MY SENIOR ARARAGI !!

Tell me...
Hasn't any-thing...
odd happened today...?
No ...?
Not really?
Just you!!
Well, the skills test is coming up
and that's giving me a head-ache.
In fact, I'm going to a study session today.
A study session ?

There's someone in my class with ridiculously good grades...
so I'm gonna get tutored, one-on-one.
It's more like a home tutor.
You know I'm a washout. I'm not in a great spot.
Hm ...
Oh, I know!
PNN
You're talking about my senior Senjogahara, RIGHT?
SHRIK

Who else could it be if it's someone with good grades in your class?
You know her ...?
I've heard rumors about her.
because hidden in them was a powerful sense that something was wrong.
I should have taken notes on every last one of Kanbaru's never-ending words...
Thinking back on it,
May fortune smile on you!!
Well, I'll be off, my senior Araragi.

Someone with good grades in my class— if that's the criteria, the standout choice wouldn't be Senjogahara,
Absolute Undisputed #1
but Hanekawa ... right?
So then why did Senjogahara's name come up all of a sudden ...?
Top-class
Then, there was what Hanekawa had told me
about Kanbaru and Senjogahara's "relationship"...
I shouldn't judge based on rumor alone,
One of her juniors was super fast, too.
but at the very least
it sounded like they were pretty close in middle school...
They were known as the Valhalla Duo, you see...
And yet she'd only "heard rumors" ...?
That sounds pretty distant. Or maybe...

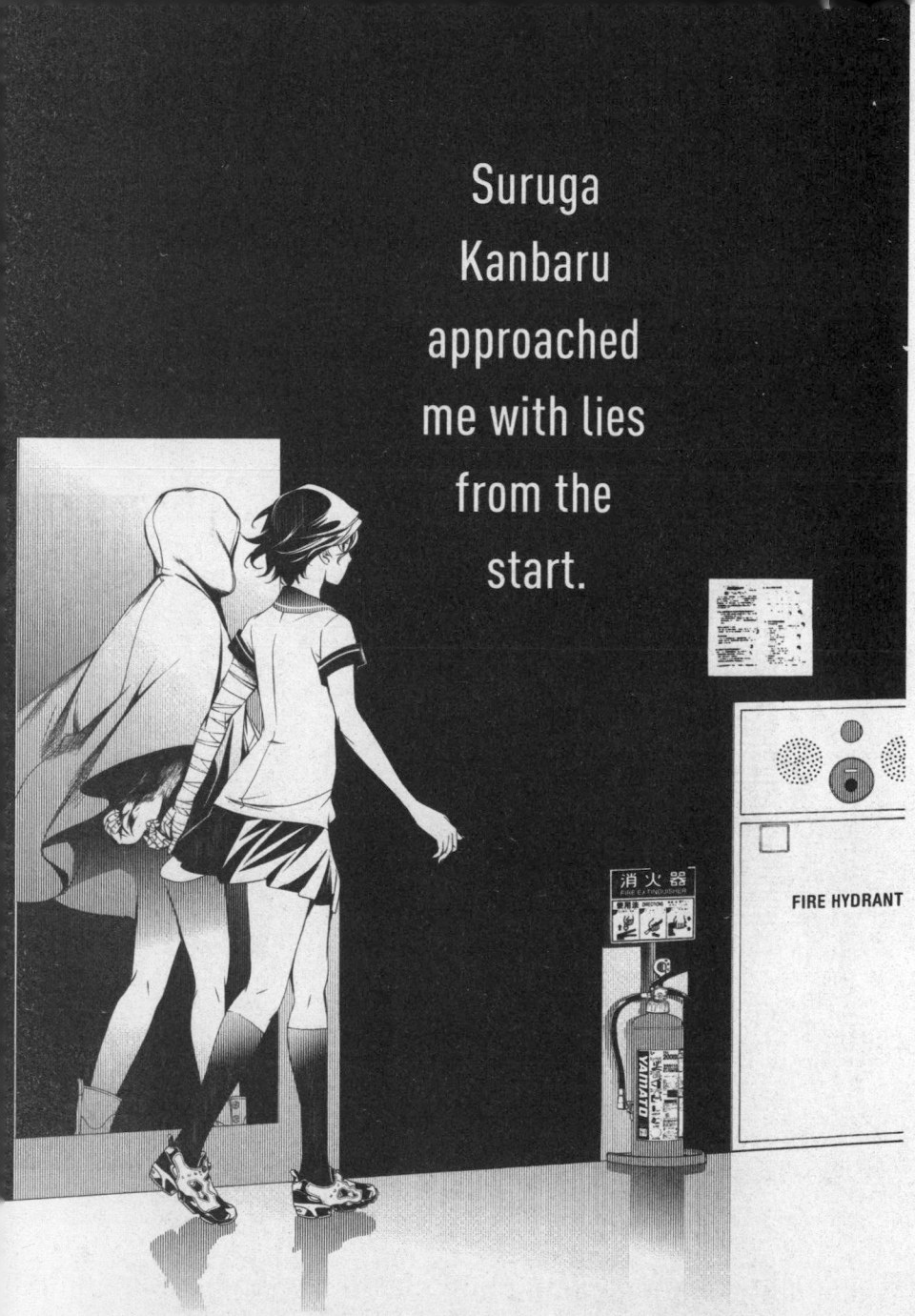
Suruga Kanbaru approached me with lies from the start.
消火器
FIRE HYDRANT

化 *bake*

物 *mono*

*SURUGAmonkey*

4

語 *gatari*

Well, I guess she's going easy on me today...
haah...
THMP.
WHP
SHP SHP
Hm?
Huh ?!
What ?
That note from Hanekawa!!
It's gone... where'd I put it?!

HERE YOU GO! ♡
This, right?
Studying Long English Passages
Mini "College English Grammar" and Expression Questions
2,000 College Entrance Exam Japanese Questions
Deeper Into Reading Aloud, Modern Japanese Lit.
Crash Course Sentences and Practice Vocab Edition
Focus Gold Vocab 1 + 2
New High School Biology Textbook by Shin Tokinori and Tokio Tsumaki
Actual Chemistry Questions: Basic Chemistry and Chemistry
Actual Physics Questions: Basic Physics and Physics
Common Japanese History B Questions and Answers
World History B Questions and Answers
Terminology Questions
Getting Unbelievable Scores on the Center Exams: Geography B, 2nd
Interview Seminar: Center Exam Modern Society and Economy
Center Exam Past Question Review
Organizing Thoughts by Shigehiro Yayama
Japanese Composition Technique by Katsuhiko Honda
Think and Grow Rich by N. Hill
A World History by William Manchester
How to Win Friends and Influence People by Dale Carnegie
SIGGLE
Since I had to borrow books from the library for the skills test
but didn't even know what to get... Hanekawa made me that list.
No worries. I had something to do in the library, anyway.
Hane-kawa...
sorry about that.
See ya, Hane-kawa! Thanks!
WHOOSH
FLUTTER
Oh...
so that's when I dropped it...

I still didn't have the courage... to show her a side of me that's so lame.
as her boy-friend,
Though I probably should've asked Senjogahara for that,

AREN'T YOU MISTER POPULAR, ARARAGI?
As of late♡

... It's not what you think.
Kanbaru's been stalking me and talking nonstop for three days now,
but I don't know what she's talking about...
and, honestly, I don't know what she wants from me.

Isn't there an easy answer sitting right there?
I'm quite sure Miss Kanbaru straight-up told you she likes you.
She was listening ?!
Well, I can't blame her given how loud we were talking...

This, and this, and...
I'm not a dating sim protagonist. It's not like I'm going to wake up one day and suddenly have girls all over me...
There's no way. That was just a figure of speech.

You're right.
Because if you were a dating sim protagonist, I'm sure I'd be one of your targets.

Huh?
Hanekawa knows about dating sims...?
Wait ...
hunh?
...
I'll have to respectfully decline.
PHYSICS
...
OKAY. THAT'S EVERY-THING.
CLAP
CLAP

JUMP
WHOOMP
But
She's the type whose kindness fools you into thinking that you're getting close to her...
only to discover that you haven't gotten any closer at all.
I don't know. Maybe...
Eh.
Don't you think?
if I were in a dating sim, I'm sure I'd be a difficult character to woo.

MAYBE SHE SAW YOU PICKING AN ABANDONED CAT OFF THE STREET?

I've never done that!
In fact, I've never even seen an abandoned cat.

Well, whatever the case, there's nothing between me and Kanbaru.
Really? I've heard she's very guarded when it comes to romance.
Which reminds me... rumor has it that Kanbaru goes from one wild romance to the next...
Today is
Return date
5/19
5/31

PSSHT
HMPH
Would a cat plunked in a cardboard box just sit in place to begin with?
That would be one well-trained cat.
PLEASE ADOPT M
Besides,
You don't like them?
I'm afraid of cats.
No...
I don't *not* like them.
They're just scary ... that's all.

# Golden Week. The cat aberration.

I mean, that's how you fell in love with Miss Senjogahara, RIIIIIIGHT? ♫

What're you, a grade schooler?

By the way, the fact that Senjogahara and I were going out
was public knowledge at that point.

HEE HEE HEE ♥
So, what will you do, Araragi?
It looks like she's still trying to figure out where you stand, but Miss Kanbaru might confess her feelings to you in the near future, you know.
...
Since I wasn't the type to be gossiped about and Senjogahara had the unique position of being "just there" in class— as natural as the air—
no one really made jokes at our expense.
WHISPER
No way.
You're enjoying this, aren't you? What is it you want to say, anyway?
I'm not feeling guilty about anything, you know. Not at all.

Huh ...
I never expected to hear you talk about feeling guilty.
It looks like you and Miss Senjo-gahara are getting along well...
and you seem to have grown up a bit, too.
Huh?
Grew up?
...?
What does that have to do with me talking about guilt?

The Japanese word for "guilt" comes from a phrase
that means "the pain of eyes fixed on your back."
Eyes fixed on your back ...
or, in other words, the sense that people are watching your every move.
We control ourselves when we're conscious of that—so they say.
"Active solitude," was it?
Not too long ago, you put up walls between yourself and others
and didn't care how people saw you.

they seemed to snag on *something* inside me.
for some reason
When Hanekawa said those words in her usual chatty way,
That's right.
Heh... Well, it's not like anyone's going to pay attention to me in the first place.
Anyway,
you really do know everything, Hanekawa...
There was me, a guy who tried to keep himself isolated...
WHY SO HEAVY?!
THOOMP
*and then there was someone totally different.*
*My polar opposite.*
Who was always in the spotlight.
I don't know everything.
I just know what I know.

A REPRESENTATIVE
OF THE MASSES,
DRAWING
EVERYONE'S
ATTENTION.

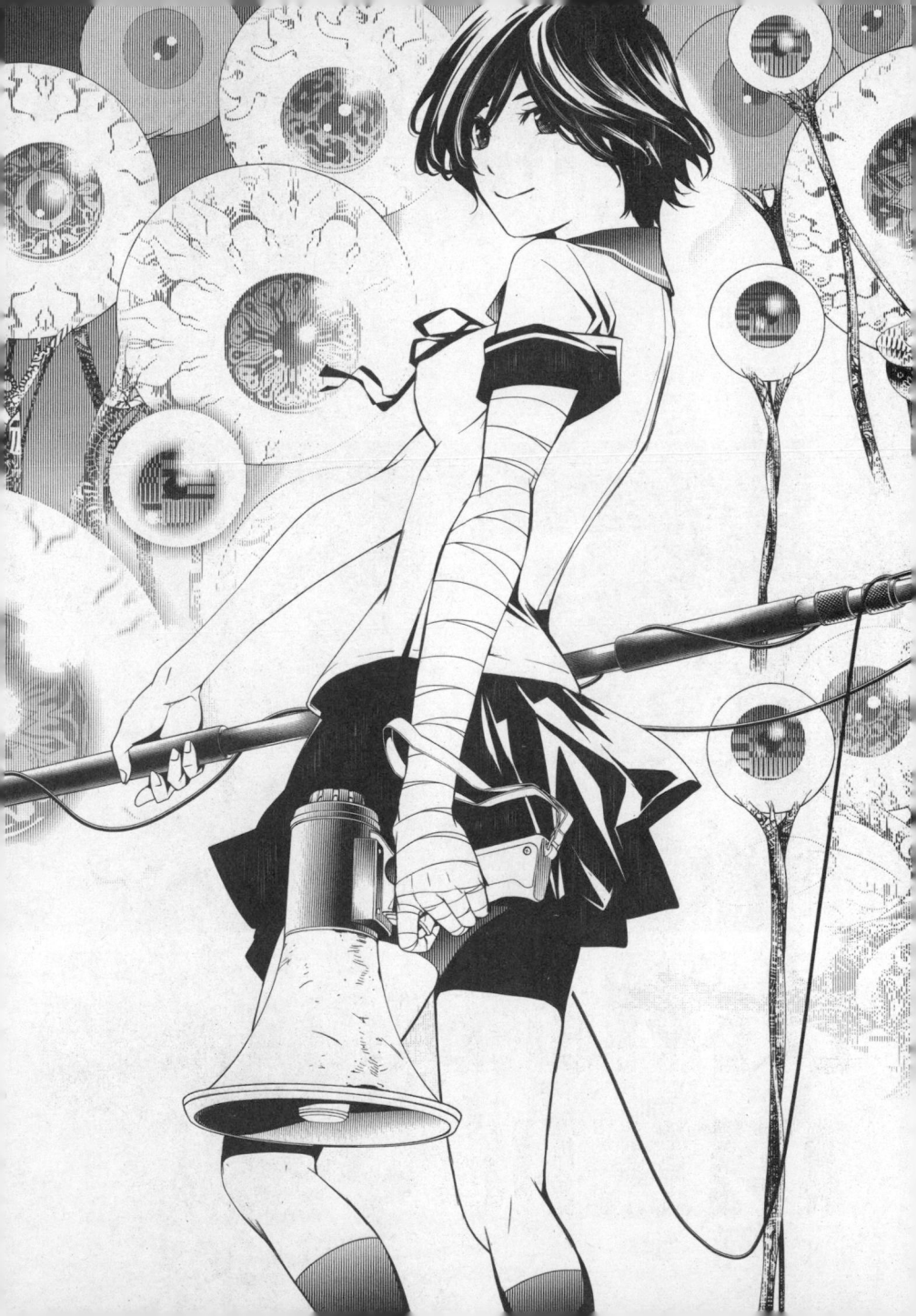

The masses, huh.
If that were me, I'd feel like...
a prisoner.
In a prison with hard walls
made from other people's eyes.

Suruga Kan-baru
is my oppo-site.
The me on the other side of the mirror.
why I had a hard time around her— why I ran.
I felt like I started to understand
When I realized that,
It should be solved...
It should be, but...
...
I know.
It's not solved at all. He still lives inside me like he was meant to be there.

Another me.

Kiss-Shot Acerola-Orion Heart-Under-Blade's thrall.

The me who is a king of aberrations.

It'd make a lot more sense to assume that Kanbaru has some kind of secondary, realistic goal.
And besides ...
...
Besides?
TWING
I've already cleared the most difficult character of all.

I feel like someone said something unpleasant about me.
That night.
May 19, 7:37 p.m.
Huh ...?
Like what ?
...

BAKE
MONO
GA
TARI
14

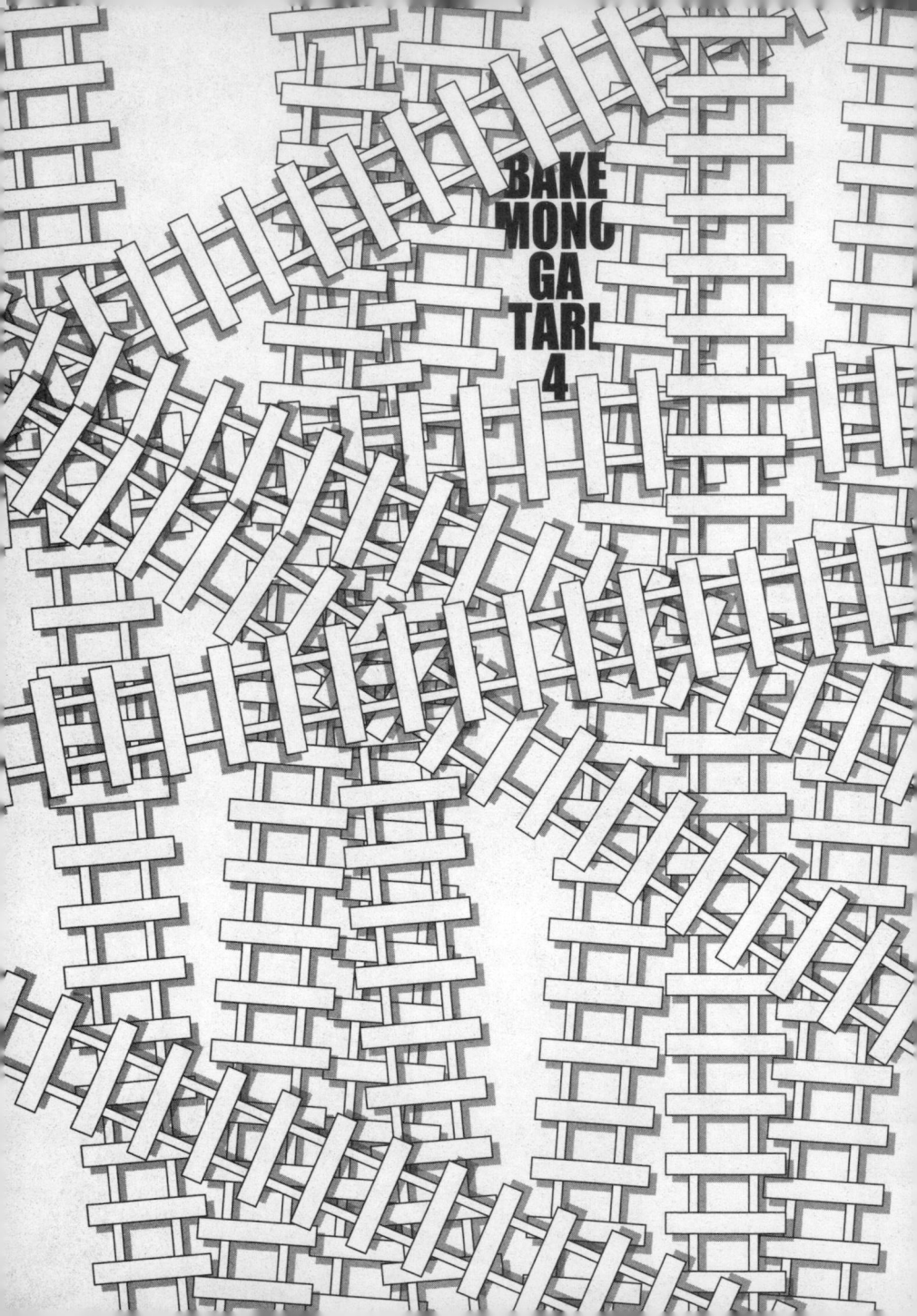
BAKE
MONO
GA
TARI
4

I feel like someone said something unpleasant about me.
GLUB GLUB
It's fine, though...
Even so,
teaching is rather difficult...
...What is she doing?
She's talking to herself...?
Well, that took me off guard...
GOLDFI

Apt. 201 of the Tamikura Apartments.
Alone with Senjogahara, studying at her place.
Yes... just the two of us.
All alone.
Senjogahara is what you'd call the only child of a single-father household...
and her father's always so busy with work...
that he doesn't get home until late...!

And yet ...
Why am I studying right now...?
GOLDFISH Shark
Hm ?
Because you're stupid?
WHAT A MEAN WAY TO PUT IT!
Even though we're going out,
we haven't done anything sexual.
Huh?!
Come to think of it, we haven't even gone on a date!
Huh

I've never struggled when it came to my studies, Araragi,
so I don't have the slightest idea why you're stuck and what's giving you trouble.
...
Oh...
Ouch...
I wonder, are you acting like you don't get it in an attempt to make me laugh?
LIKE I'D GO THAT FAR!
Oh...? Is this the only way you can maintain your pride?
I can't imagine what it's like to be the biggest fish in the smallest pond.
THE SMALL-EST? EXCUSE ME?!

But I must say,
I'm feeling motivated to help you pass this skills test
so I can grow as a person.
...
There are other things you ought to do first if you want to grow as a person...
A lot of things. Yeah, a whole lot...
Oh, be quiet.
I've strangled you to death.
The present perfect tense ?!
AM I ALREADY DEAD?!
This is my second time coming here... the first being eleven days ago...
which means...

I can't help but remember it...
BZZZ
BZZZ
SEARCH
FLASH
Off Guard Search
CHECK FOR OPENINGS

Just thinking about how your difficulty is set to hard...
Nothing.
What?
Openings not detected...
I can't tell if her guard is all the way down, or if it's as high as it can get...
By the way, Araragi, I was wondering...
what are you going to do next?
GRIT
Huh?
I'd like to start off by eating a home-cooked meal made by you!!
TWITCH
Huh?
Oh, that...
Oh...
After you graduate.

I don't really like any of that terminology because it's an oversimplification of a real issue, but of course, your own views and wishes take precedence. Oh, but I suppose you could always learn a trade at a vocational school to start off?
You're at the end of your second month of your last year of high school. You must have given it at least a little bit of thought. I know you said something along the lines of only caring about making it to graduation, but does that mean you're going to find a job right away? Do you have some sort of concrete plan? A connection or an in at some company? Are you going to be a temp at first? Or maybe you'll just be a NEET?

I'M YOUR GIRL-FRIEND.

What are you, my mother...?
Your mother ?
What are you talking about?

true.
Uh... well,
GOLDFISH
I would like to walk the same path as you if I can.
Huh?
I was happy to hear that...
But...
you're going to go to college, right?
Yes.
I am.
Well...
that'd be... a little...
What's the term? Physically impossible...?
Right...
Ignorance may be a crime,
but stupidity isn't.
SUPER STUDY CHEMISTRY
Hm?

It's not a crime, it's a punish-ment.
For what?
A punish-ment?
馬鹿の業
The Wages of Stupidity
Miss Senjogahara now had a clear idea of how the ant felt when it watched the grasshopper freeze to death.
You poor thing... If you had been more virtuous in your past life like me, this wouldn't have happened.
See? It's even in this book.

Heh heh heh ...
I have to hand it to you, Araragi... getting me to identify with a bug is no small feat.
...
Just endure it...
Calm yourself down by counting prime numbers ...
That's right. Think of prime numbers ...
Stupid
Stupid
Stupid
Stupid
Retorting here will only cause the knife to cut deeper.
Why not just let it go and drop dead?
Even a grasshopper becomes useful as a carcass when the ant deigns to feed on its nutrients.
THE NEXT TIME WE MEET, IT'LL BE IN COURT!!!

SIGH
...
It's no good...
I've never had a girlfriend before,
I'm so nervous that I might piss my pants ...
TREMBLE
TREMBLE
TREMBLE
so I don't know what to do in a situation like this...

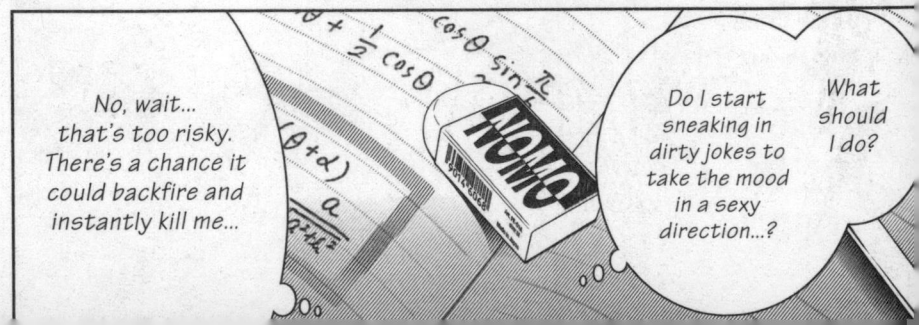
No, wait... that's too risky. There's a chance it could backfire and instantly kill me...
Do I start sneaking in dirty jokes to take the mood in a sexy direction...?
What should I do?

SHOULD WE LIVE TOGETHER AFTER WE GRADUATE?
BWAP
Fire!
BOOM

Not a bad idea?
I don't like your tone.
...
Well, that's not a bad idea.
Yes... I'd like to.
Please, let's do that.
Oh, I see.
SKRIBB
SKRIBB
SKRIBB
SKRIBB

This girl...
...
is not the type to joke at moments like this... Even someone as unobservant as me can see that by now.
This is Hitagi Senjogahara I'm dealing with.
KLANG
KLANG
KLANG
KLANG
KLANG
...
But maybe ...
Two years. Hitagi Senjogahara avoided contact with other people for two years.
...
TWITCH
SKRIBB
Chart Style

Maybe Senjogahara is just as clueless as I am about what to do in a moment like this.

What is it?
Hey, Senjo-gahara?
Oh, right. Two years ago would mean...
You know Kanbaru, right?

Understanding
English Sentences
PART I
No.
DATE
No.
DATE

Chemistry Basics included
CHEMISTRY
SUPER
STUDY
CHEMISTRY SUPER STUDY

Kan-baru?
What about that girl, Araragi?
You sound awfully close to her.

Kan-baru?
GOLDFISH Shark
Is there some-thing be-tween you and that girl, Araragi?
H-
Hey! Hey !!

FWOOM
FWOOM
FWOOM
The God of Jealousy

FWOOM

It's a funny story. Yes, Kanbaru was...
my junior in middle school.
I was on the track team.
She was on the basket-ball team.
We did different activities, but we knew each other as the respective star of those teams.
She made me do all sorts of things for her
—she did.
In our private lives as well... in all sorts of ways.
So why do you ask, Araragi?

GOLDFISH
Shark
I can hear it dripping from the way you say her name.
NO, NO! IT'S NOT DRIPPING! IT'S NOT EVEN DAMP!!
"I'M TOTALLY CLOSER TO KANBARU. OH, WAIT, THAT REMINDS ME. DIDN'T YOU, LIKE, SAY YOU KNOW HER OR SOMETHING?"
You're
like

I got to see this side of her over something I have a good excuse for.
Just how jealous is this girl...?
In a way... I'm glad.

STOP, NO! LOSING AN EYEBALL WOULD STILL BE BAD!!
So a single eyeball can't be that bad, can it?
You heal from injuries incredibly fast.

Oh, am I?
I like how those words make me feel.

SST

YOU'RE THE ONLY GIRL FOR ME, SENJO-GAHA-RA!!!
I DON'T FEEL GUILTY ABOUT ANY-THING !!!

THP
DRIP
DRIP
You licked it, idn't you, Ara-agi?
I made sure not to spill any.
BOMP
BOMP

Ya know, you're going to kill someone one of these days...
STOP MAKING UP ABILITIES I DON'T EVEN HAVE!!
Your quick powers of judgment let you turn a crisis into an opportunity, even in this situation. Go ahead, you should be proud of that.
In a way, I'd say that's worthy o respect. You're trying this hard to make me change clothes so you can sneal a peek.
GOLDFISH Shark
DON'T TRY TO MAKE SOMETHING DISTURBING SOUND COOL!
I won't choose anyone else, I promise.
You'll be my first.
And when I do, I'll make sure it's you.

Winter, a Time of Ends
—The Steamy Murder at the Naoetsu Hot Springs—
Her deep love leads to...
To be loved to death...
to be killed by the one you love—could there be any better way to die?
I'D RATHER PASS ON A TWISTED LOVE LIKE THAT!!
y 29 Premiere
Hm?
Oh, uh.
Yeah ... I guess.
WHAT A VAGUE ANSWER!
Really? That's too bad.
And surprising. If it were by your hands, Araragi—
You wouldn't mind being killed?

What's the big deal?
If I were to kill you, Araragi,
I suppose I would mind, actually.
Well, um... yes.
FOLLOWED BY A VAGUE REFUSAL!!
What?
I won't have that.
Winter, a Time of Ends 2
—The Woman Who Cries at Takada Castle in Joe
NO MATTER WHO KILLS ME IN WHAT WAY, ANYTHING IS BETTER THAN GETTING KILLED BY YOU!
NO!
I would be by your side during your final moments. Isn't that romantic?
May 3 Premiere

If anyone ever kills you, Araragi...

Aren't promises meant to be broken?

I'll kill who did it.

So,
that girl... We were talking about Suruga Kanbaru, right?
Oh ...
Yeah...
She's been, like ...
weirdly following me around for about three days now...
...
Hm... I see...

Hey, Araragi?
What's flooded on top and in blazes on the bottom?
What...? Oh, I know that one.
A cauldron... right?
A riddle?
WHAT ARE YOU PLANNING TO DO TO THE HOME OF THE SCHOOL'S BASKETBALL STAR?!
IT'S KAN-BARU'S HOUSE.
BZZT.
Oh, I'm just kidding...
I don't know... When she says it,
it doesn't sound like a joke...
...
One year ago.

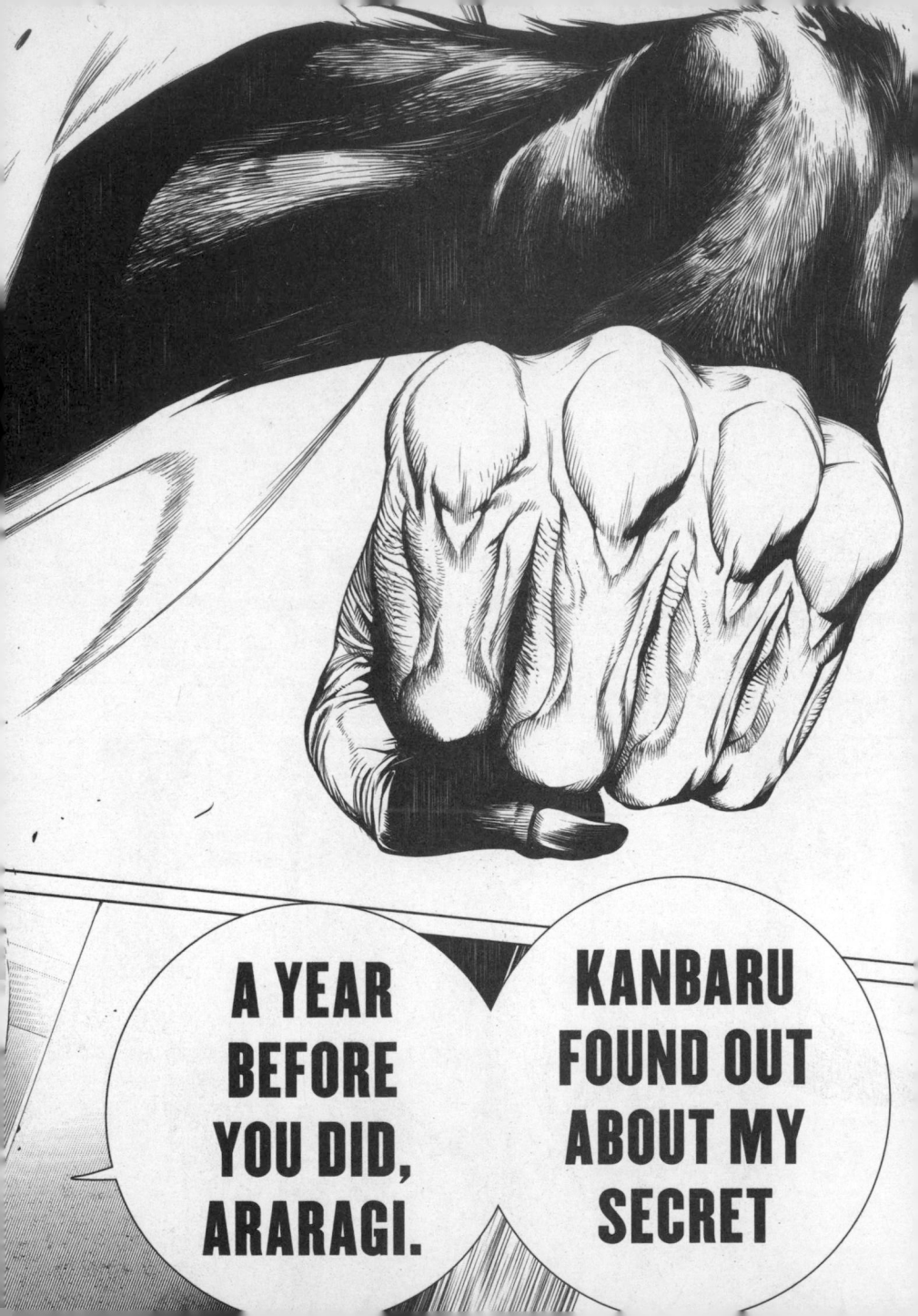
A YEAR BEFORE YOU DID, ARARAGI.
KANBARU FOUND OUT ABOUT MY SECRET

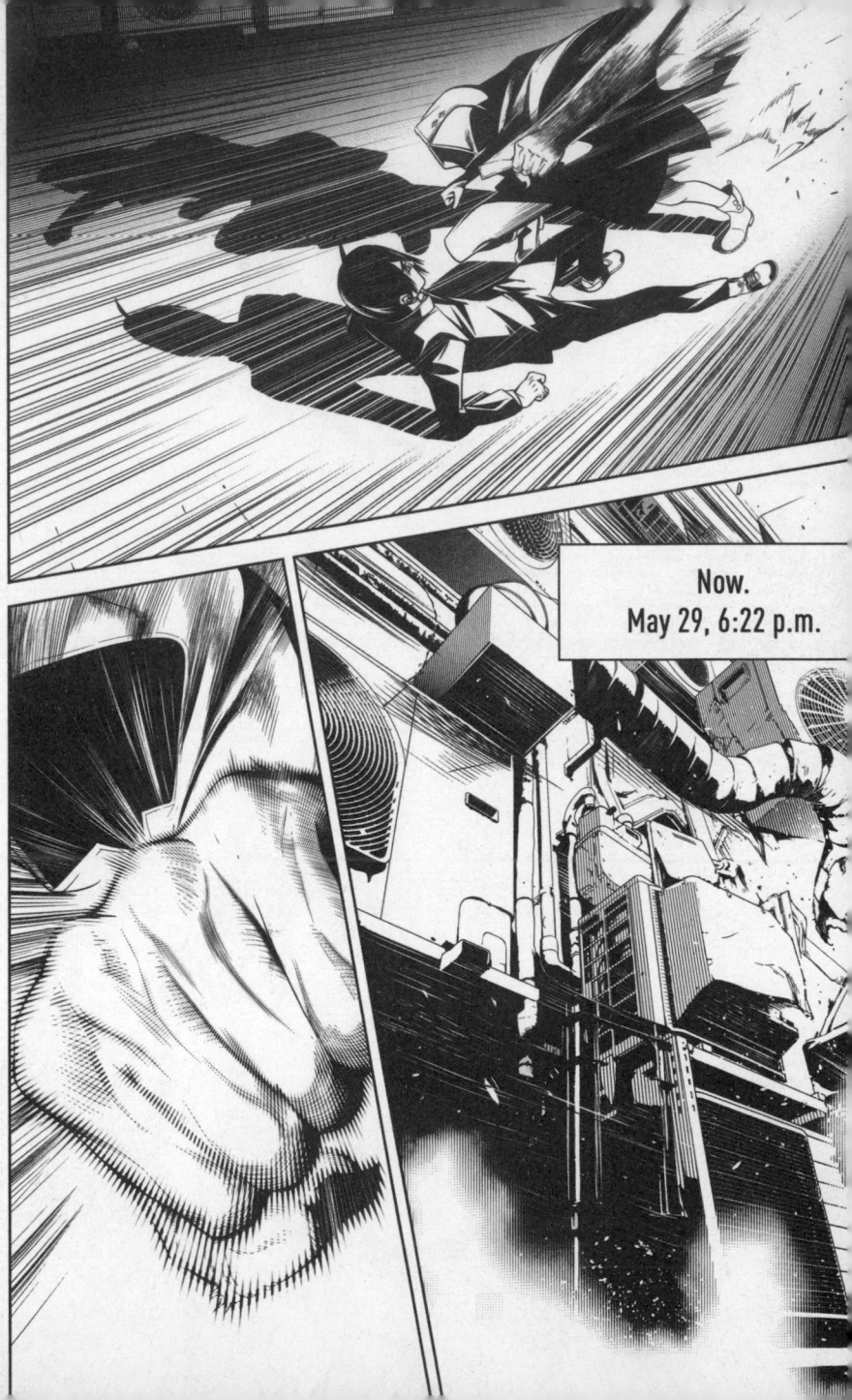
Now.
May 29, 6:22 p.m.

GRAB
THWAKK
KWRRR

In that case... I bet she tried to save you, knowing her.
She did.
But, of course ...
I refused.
ZSH
Now we're complete strangers.
We were, yes.
You were friends ... weren't you?
...
KREAK

SWZZT
KSHT
KSHT
KSHT
But you... tried to get involved with me anyway ...
I dealt with her in a *similar way* I dealt with you.

SKRRCH
SKRRCH
FSSSH
FSSSH
FSSSH
SKRRCH
FSSSH
FSSSH
Oh...

SKRRCH
FSSSSH
FSSSSH
SKRRCH
SKRRCH
SKRCH
I get it.
I think I know how she feels.
Kanbaru never came back.
That was all our relationship amounted to.

Hey, Kan-baru.
You wanted to be me, didn't you?

物 *mono*

*SURUGAmonkey*

4

話 *gatari*

化 *bake*

化 bake

物 mono

SURUGAmonkey

4

語 gatari

I was some-one
Kanbaru looked up to, if I do say so myself.
First off, close the door, at least when you're changing.
It doesn't close right.
Do you want to try? Actually, I'd prefer if you broke it. With the money you'd have to pay us, we'd be able to fix it.
RATTLE
RATTLE

Yes...
it seems that girl
hasn't forgotten me, after all.

Though we were in different clubs in middle school ...
she still came to watch my meets and even acted like the team's manager ...
Oh...

In other words, a part of Senjogahara had encouraged that behavior.
She was trying to play the role of a character in *a position like that.*

She wanted to always be untouchable, perfect, flawless. It must have been during that time.
It was something she did for her mother, who had fallen prey to that cult.
It's true.
Sorry for the trouble, Araragi.
This is on me for not being able to liquidate my relationships.
Liqui-date ...?
When she says it, the word sounds ice-cold...
Senjogahara used an unnatural, awful-sounding word.

May
日/SUN
月/MON
We started dating five days ago, and the stalking started three days ago. So the timing seems to work out.
Kanbaru must have heard we're going out.
Senjogahara falls
Start dating Senjogahara
Snail
Someone begins stalking me
First study session

I really wasn't who she was after.
That much I knew, but something still didn't feel right...

Um ...
so what are you trying to say?
That she's curious about what kind of guy Hitagi Senjogahara's boyfriend is... and she's checking me out?
GOLDFISH
Shark

YOU HAVE SUCCEEDED WHERE SHE FAILED.
LOW CLEARANCE
That's more than enough reason... as far as she'd be concerned.
...

The way she incessantly praised me might have been closer to how she really felt than I'd expected...
Oh... so that's what it is.
But in that case, things are different now, Senjo-gahara ...
You know, we cleared up that secret of yours, so—
GOLDFISH Shark
I don't think she's being malicious or anything.
She's annoying.
Didn't I tell you already?
I was playing a character back then.

I won't go back to any of that, and I don't see any need to.
With that, Senjogahara put an end to our conversation.
That's how I've decided to live my life.

ZING
KSHH
I wonder
what happened between
Kanbaru and Senjo-gahara ...
KLANG
C-TWO

I have a feeling that dealing with her in a "similar way" wasn't enough ...
カシャ KSHT
I dealt with her in a similar way I dealt with you.
カシャ KSHT
URP
BLG CH
Since Kanbaru deeply admired and respected her,
I bet Senjogahara's rejection was hair-raisingly intense—completely different from the one I'd experienced.

In other words... you're the second to know.
The only other person at this school who knows about this is the health teacher, Harukami...
Senjogahara once told me that the only other person
at this school who knows about this is the health teacher, Harukami.
You'v no-tice righ ?
The secret about my body.
...
How did that make Kanbaru feel?
...
She's incredibly fast, but...

I did not understand.
BOOM
BWOOSH
TOSHIBA

She wouldn't even tolerate her existence.
Kanbaru had been forced... *to forget it all.* How could I understand how she'd feel...?
ゴオオ
GROOOAR

GAFWOOSH
FWOOSH
FWOOSH

She only has two attack patterns. She either jumps in with a straight or a hook ...
She still moves too quickly to see...
SKRRK
SKRRK
But no matter how quick she is,
SKRR SKRR SKRR
SUPERSONIC
she isn't faster than the speed of sound.

FWOOSH
SGRRK
SKRR
SKRR
SKRR
SKRR
SKRR

They squeak every time she throws a punch.
Though showing up in rubber boots was a total mistake.
Maybe she's trying to hide her identity ...?
BOMF
She punches in a straight line... and only using her left hand.
NO TRESPASSING
I just have to move when I hear her boots squeak and I won't get hit.
WHAKK
KAN-BARU.

TWITCH
PTT
If you're Kanbaru, then I have no reason to fight you...
how-ever.

There's even less of a reason for me to run away.

I probably shouldn't
butt into problems like this...
She says she won't go back
and doesn't need to, huh...
Senjo-gahara's not the type who can act selfishly enough
to try to get back with an old flame she harshly rejected just because her own misfortunes were solved.

BWOOSH
BOOM
You're both a little too awkward.
And so...
I won't give my two cents,
but I will give you my fist.

THROB
KRK
KRK
KRK
!!
FSSK
FWOOSH
BAM

BOOM
SKRR
ZHTT

I was lucky that she *just so happened* to attack me that day.
I let Shinobu drink my blood the day prior,
so I was closer to being a vampire than usual.
If that had happened two days ago,
I imagine I'd long be immobile.
BFOH

A predict-able, swing-ing
upper hook.
PTT
She was staring a hole into me...
but what I went for is...
GLAAARE

SGGT
BEER
BEER
KRAASH
BEER
BEER

BOMB

BOOM

The Valhalla Duo?
WATCH OUT!!
DON'T COME IN.
NO
禁止
立入
TRESPASSING
KHAA
カハッ
Do you have a minute ...?
I wanted to ask you something.
That's right, Hanekawa.
Re-zoning Ahead
Thank you for your cooperation

10 minutes earlier.
May 29, 6:12 p.m.
Hm? Sure. I was just doing some light studying anyway.
Hanekawa
End Call
Right before that raincoat attacked me,
I just so happened to be corrob-orating evidence on Kanbaru with Hanekawa.
Well... it wasn't like I came into physical contact with them just because we went to the same middle school, you know.
Those two were celebrities, so frumpy old yours truly just knew about them, even if they didn't know about me...
You mentioned something before.
You said Senjogahara and Kanbaru were called the Valhalla Duo, right?

Though I was moved by Hanekawa's humble and off-the-mark stance...
the term Valhalla apparently comes from Norse mythology. It's the heavenly hall where gods reside, and where the spirits of fallen heroes are welcome.

Plus, Kanbaru's name starts with the character for "god" and Senjogahara's with the ones for "battlefield." Thus, the Valhalla Duo.
Kanbaru's "baru" and Senjogahara's "hara" makes "*baruhara*," which is Japanese for "Valhalla."
I see.
You couldn't hope for a more snug fit. There must have been someone real witty at school.

Yes.
Senjogahara... was different then, right?
PM7 : 02
They were close.
Very close.
In fact, I think you could compare her to present-day Kanbaru. She was the star of the academy.
everyone revered her, whether they were her juniors or seniors...
It wasn't just Kanbaru,
Though she seems
to be changing again, bit by bit.

I think so too.
Yeah, ...
As her boyfriend, I wanted to say "That's because she's going out with me."
But that was a little... No, it was *totally* wrong.
It's not that she changed. She was just going *back to the way she once was.*
To who she was before she met the crab aberration— and even before that.
Not the Hitagi with a forcefield around her and acting like a superhuman...
but the *original* Hitagi Senjo-gahara.

So...
So that's why I couldn't help think-ing,
I want Senjo-gahara to find what she lost.
I want her to take back what she threw away.
I won't go back to any of that, and I don't see any need to.
there isn't much of her left.
GRRT
Even if...

'Cuz that
is some-thing ... I can never do ...

I'm really aiming
for those beer bottles scattered on the ground...

and those shards !!
We might call ourselves a couple, but I don't think either of us knows what it really means to "go out."
Heh ...
Heh ...
Heh ...
Heh ...
ZMM
ZMM
ZMM

If *this* is a byproduct of dating—something that comes with the territory—
then fine.
I'll see it through to the end.
I'll start
by keeping her from rushing forward. I'll take out her legs ...!!

TMP

BSSHT
Heh

I knew it.
That's why I ran you into this place.
Aber-rations *think in a very logical way.*
With her special abilities, there is no difference between the ground and the walls!
The ground is covered with shards of glass, and the wall has plenty of footing.
SKRRR
Reason would state... she picks the latter.

If she's in the air, her ability to sprint
won't mean a thing.
GRRT
ZSH

WOOM
Kan-baru!!
Sorry for being kinda rough... but you've got to calm down
so we can talk!!!
ZSH

BOOM
GRRT
GRRT
BRRIP
GRRT
GRRT
GRRT
BRRRIP
BRRRIP
BRRRIP
BRRRIP

"Aberrations are faithful to reason."
In the blink of an eye,
I knew what she was going to do...
SHUDDER

# After all, we're both monsters.

BOOM

But that was an excuse.
Just one of them would've easily sent a person to the hospital.
If I had moved, the fragments would've flown past me like shotgun pellets.
was to keep her from seeing me fight in this form.
All I wanted

No, wait...
What will I do next...?!
Damn... I didn't think this through at all...
SST
TWITCH
DASH
コッ
THOK

Good evening, Araragi.
But I'll let you off easy, given how you look. You're half-forgiven.
You're very late for our second study session and didn't contact me once. You deserve to die a thousand times over.
I'd say.
Hey, Senjo-gahara ... it's been a while.

WHY WOULD A CONVOY OF TRUCKS PASS THROUGH HERE?!
It's very admirable that you'd go so far as to have a convoy of trucks run over you as a form of self-punishment.
OOF!
KOFF KOFF !
VROOM

Do you remember their license plates? I'll go and avenge you.
No, I just tripped and fell.
I'll start by turning the cars into scrap metal, then put the drivers through so much pain that they'll beg me to finish them by running over them repeatedly with a bicycle.
Just look around. The road's all bumpy from construction, right...?

Whew... Judging by the way she's acting,
it seems like she couldn't see us fighting from where she came in...
Then I think I'll pay a visit to whatever company was responsible for the sloppy construction here. I have a blade delivery for them.
It's fine... I'll be able to move if I just rest a bit longer...
Oh.
Okay, then. I'll reward you with a very special something.
TUG
ひょいっ
FWOOSH

You don't need me to call an ambulance, do you?
Though you must be in pain.
Um ...
Is she trying to cheer me up
to help ease my pain...?
I think so.
If she came for me, unable to wait any longer when I no-showed the study session I had promised,
then that is something I'm very happy about.

But
the smell of a beast still hung in the air.
Maybe
I should con-fess.
Back then ...
when I realized the beast's intentions, in that moment ...
I
didn't care anymore.

I wanted to brawl like the beast that I am and indulge in the blood-shed.

Maybe I should confess that those uncon-trollable urges ran through me.

The next day,
This is a rare opportunity, so I should take a good look.
I paid a visit to Kanbaru's house.

Continued in Volume 5

There are sudden glimpses of Suruga's shadow.
BAKEMONOGATARI 5
A surprise attack by an unknown aberration.
Preview

Next Volume
What "wish" did she make when the two came together?
The truth behind "Suruga Monkey."
VOLUME 5 AVAILABLE NOW!
Ah.
All right.
To business, then.

# BAKEMONOGATARI

## volume 4

A Vertical Comics Edition

Editing: Kristi Fernandez
Translation: Ko Ransom
Production: Grace Lu
Hiroko Mizuno

© 2019 NISIOISIN, Oh!great
All rights reserved.
First published in Japan in 2019 by Kodansha, Ltd., Tokyo
Publication for this English edition arranged through Kodansha, Ltd., Tokyo
English language version produced by Vertical Comics,
an imprint of Kodansha USA Publishing, LLC

Translation provided by Vertical Comics, 2020
Published by Kodansha USA Publishing, LLC, New York

Originally published in Japanese as *BAKEMONOGATARI 4* by Kodansha, Ltd.
*BAKEMONOGATARI* first serialized in *Weekly Shonen Magazine*,
Kodansha, Ltd., 2017-

This is a work of fiction.

ISBN: 978-1-949980-40-0

Manufactured in the United States of America

First Edition

Third Printing

Kodansha USA Publishing, LLC
451 Park Avenue South
7th Floor
New York, NY 10016
www.kodansha.us

Vertical books are distributed through Penguin-Random House Publisher Services.